**BOXeR**
FUN IS OUR BUSINESS

www.booksbyboxer.com

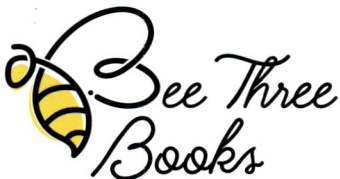

*Bee Three Books*

Bee Three Publishing is an imprint of Books By Boxer
Published by
Books By Boxer, Leeds, LS13 4BS, UK
Books by Boxer (EU), Dublin, D02 P593, IRELAND
Boxer Gifts LLC, 955 Sawtooth Oak Cir, VA 22802, USA
© Books By Boxer 2025
cs@boxer.gifts
All Rights Reserved
**MADE IN CHINA**
ISBN: 9781915410856

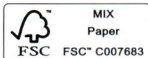

MIX
Paper
FSC   FSC™ C007683

This book is produced from responsibly sourced paper to ensure forest management

# CAN DOGS BE AWARDED MILITARY MEDALS?

In 1941 a military medal with an unlikely recipient was found in a house in Bristol, England. The Blue Cross Medal was found with an inscription detailing how the awardee, a Great Dane called Juliana, put out an incendiary bomb that the Luftwaffe had dropped on her owner's home.

The method? Peeing on it. In fact, Juliana had received not one, but TWO Blue Cross Medals, the second being for alerting her owner to a fire that broke out in his shoe shop. What a daring Dane!

# WHAT MADE ALEXANDER SO GREAT?

It was widely documented that after death his body remained unchanged for the 6 days it took to prepare him for burial. To the ancient Greeks, this confirmed he was a God - which was pretty great to them!

But there might be another, more realistic theory; he wasn't dead. His symptoms align with a disease called Guillain-Barré Syndrome, which along with paralysis of the body, may lead to the body requiring less oxygen, making his breath virtually undetectable.

Unfortunately for Alex, in those days it was an absence of breath rather than pulse which led to the declaration of death. So, the bigger question is... was Alexander the Great buried alive?

# WHAT IS THE WORST FORM OF EXECUTION?

The usual hanging or beheading looks quite pale compared to this form of execution... which was done by elephant! In South and Southeast Asia, elephants were trained to kill by crushing, dismembering, and even torturing victims over time.

There are written accounts of executions in Siam (now known as Thailand) where elephants used their trunks to grab someone tied to a stake, throw them in the air, and pierce them with their tusks, before stamping them to death. This form of execution was still used up into the 18th and 19th centuries - heavy stuff!

# CAN YOU BE 'ARMED TO THE TEETH'?

In the olden days, there was a high demand for dentures due to the rise of sugary diets and poor dental hygiene - a lot of teeth had to get pulled! Unfortunately, ivory dentures weren't quite working out, so people were looking for human teeth to use. Where could they get these teeth?

Well, from dead people, of course. So when the Battle of Waterloo rolled around in 1815 and thousands of soldiers' bodies lay in one location with mouths full of teeth... scavengers, and even surviving soldiers got to rummaging for teeth - and boy did they hit the jackpot!

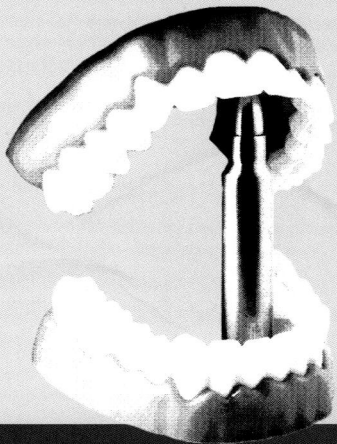

# IF A VOLCANO ERUPTS AND NOBODY IS AROUND, DOES IT MAKE A SOUND?

It certainly does in the case of Krakatoa, an uninhabited volcanic island in Indonesia, which when it erupted in 1883 created the loudest sound in history. The volcanic eruption had 13,000 times the explosive yield of the nuclear bomb used in Hiroshima.

The largest eruption of Krakatoa was heard 3,110 km away in Perth, Australia, with the acoustic pressure wave of the eruption circling the globe over three times. Despite few people being affected by the actual eruptions themselves, the tsunamis that were caused by it reached height of 79 feet, and massively contributed to the death toll of 36,417 people.

# WHAT IS 'MONKEY BUSINESS'?

James Wilde, a signalman who had lost both of his lower legs in a work accident, bought a Chacma baboon whom he named Jack. Initially, he taught Jack to push him in a trolley, to and from work. With time, Jack also learned how to change the signals himself so when trains tooted their whistle to signal a change of the tracks, Jack was able to choose the right lever.

Jack was so good at his job in fact, that when someone complained that a monkey was operating the tracks, the railway manager tested Jack's abilities, and they formally hired him. From then on, Jack was paid 20 cents a day and reportedly never made a mistake in his career - he wasn't monkeying around!

# CAN ANIMALS BE PUT ON TRIAL?

In the Middle Ages, animals were often put on trial. From rats to grasshoppers and snails, animals could face trial just as humans did: accused of crimes and sentenced to punishment if found guilty. One of history's most famous animal cases? A 3-year-old pig who was found guilty of murder by eating the face of a young child.

The pig was sentenced to death by hanging, and it's rumored that the pig was even dressed up in human clothes for the execution, and other pigs in the town were forced to watch as a warning to themselves. Oink!

# HOW FAR COULD YOU TOSS A FOX?

A brilliant question, one that aristocrats of 17th and 18th century Europe would find the answer to with their popular sport 'fox tossing', or 'Fuchsprellenin' in German. The game was played by laying a cord sling between two people stood around 20 to 25 feet apart. A fox, or other animal, was then released, and when the victim crossed the sling, the participants would pull hard on the ends to throw the animal as high as possible into the air.

Unfortunately, this brutal sport was often fatal for the animals involved, with one contest held by the King of Poland killing 647 foxes, 533 hares, 34 badgers, and 21 wildcats.

# HOW BAD IS CHOCOLATE FOR YOU, REALLY?

If there's a bomb inside, pretty bad! That's what Adolf Hitler planned to do to kill British wartime prime minister Winston Churchill. According to a letter from a high-ranking intelligence official, the Germans had planned to coat explosive devices in a thin layer of dark chocolate and wrap it in branded packaging.

This plan was devised due to Churchill's apparent love for the sweet treat, and it was hoped it could be smuggled into the War Cabinet meetings, potentially killing everyone inside. However, British spies found out about the plan and were able to foil the plot.

# CAN YOU REALLY JINX SOMETHING?

It seems like John Sedgwick managed to! Whilst overseeing the preparations for the Battle of Spotsylvania Courthouse, Confederate sharp-shooters were occasionally firing at Union troops.

When his men would duck for cover, Sedgwick laughed and said "They couldn't hit an elephant at that distance." Just moments later, a bullet hit him just below his eye, killing him instantly. Seems like he really spoke it into existence - or rather, jinxed it!

# ARE NAVIES ALWAYS THE MOST EFFECTIVE?

Apparently not! The voyage of the Russian Baltic fleet during the Russo-Japanese War is one of the most catastrophically incompetent examples of naval action in history. To summarise:

- They attacked British fishing trawlers thinking they were Japanese warships, successfully sinking one of the ships but damaging one of their own in the process.
- **Their refrigerated ship failed and dumped large amounts of rotten meat into the sea, causing sharks to follow them.**
- During a funeral in Madagascar for one of their crewmembers, they used a live round in the gunnery salute, hitting one of their own ships.

- During a gunnery practice they only managed one hit - the ship that was towing the target.
- The hospital ship (which kept its lights on during a nighttime mission, as per the rules of war), signaled to a Japanese ship to be cautious of the other Russian ships, thinking it was a Russian ship itself.
- The Battle of Tsushima ensues, with 5000 Russian deaths, and 6000 Russian prisoners captured, but only around 100 Japanese casualties.

Russia lost the war shortly after.

# HOW CAN YOU F**** AROUND AND FIND OUT?

When a band of Cilician pirates kidnapped a Roman nobleman they didn't quite understand what they had got themselves in for. The captive was charming and laughed at them when they told him his ransom was for 20 talents, suggesting that 50 talents would instead be more appropriate. He bossed them around, took part in their games, and even joked that he would have them all crucified.

When the captive was eventually released, they thought they would never see him again. But the captive raised a naval force in Miletus (where he had no public or military office), captured the pirates, then had them all crucified. The captive in question was a young Julius Caesar.

# ARE PIGEONS GOVERNMENT SPIES?

No. But they were once recruited to guide missiles for the US military! In the 1940s B. F. Skinner tacked up pigeons in harnesses and trained them to peck in grain dishes to guide the movement of a small cart.

After securing some military funding, Skinner placed three pigeons in the nose cone of a missile, with an electronic screen in front of their faces. As the pigeons pecked the target, pulleys attached to their heads guided the missile until impact. Inevitably, the pigeons would then become a waft of feathers and eventually the military decided they would be better off pursuing other avenues of missile guidance. Phew!

# WHO WOULD WIN IN A FIGHT BETWEEN THE ARMY AND EMUS?

The Great Emu War of 1932 occurred due to the large amount of destruction emus were wreaking on the lands of farmers in Western Australia. The farmers complained that the 20,000 emus, who had migrated to the area, were spoiling their crops and leaving holes in fences which allowed rabbits to enter and cause more issues.

In response, the Minister of Defence agreed to send Australian soldiers to the area, armed with machine guns. What seemed like an easy task, was in reality much more difficult, with emus deploying "guerilla tactics", splitting up into small groups which "made use of the military equipment uneconomic".

Due to the emus' ability to "face machine guns with the invulnerability of tanks", the first attempt was deemed unsuccessful, with only around 200-300 emus being killed in a single month.

The attempts continued, with increasing success, but the war was eventually abandoned in favor of putting bounties out for emus. It is widely acknowledged that the emus won the war.

# DO CATS REALLY HAVE NINE LIVES?

Whilst he didn't survive nine deadly situations, he did supposedly survive three: Unsinkable Sam was found floating on a board when German battleship, the Bismarck, was sunk in a naval battle on the 27th of May, 1941. Taken in by the crew of HMS Cossack, a British destroyer, he was given the name 'Oscar'. Oscar next survived a brush with death when the Cossack was torpedoed by a German U-boat, killing 159 of the crew - but notably no cats.

He was then transferred to the HMS Ark Royal, an aircraft carrier, which was then also torpedoed by a U-Boat. After this near-death experience, Sam was finally sent to live the rest of his days in a seaman's home in Belfast. A happy ending for a very lucky cat!

# HOW EASY IS IT TO ESTABLISH YOUR OWN SOVEREIGN NATION?

Pretty easy, it seems. In 1964, Leicester Hemingway, the younger brother of Ernest Hemingway, established his own 'micronation', named New Atlantis. How did he manage that? Well, by building a 240 sq ft bamboo raft and towing it six miles off the coast of Jamaica, of course. He then claimed his raft was an island and therefore deserved sovereignty. By 1965, there were six people living on the raft, including Hemingway's family.

With the ultimate goal of building an artificial island from the seafloor, and performing marine research, New Atlantis met its premature end after a few years when it was destroyed in tropical storms.

# IS LAUGHTER CONTAGIOUS?

It certainly was in Tanganyika (now modern Tanzania), in 1962. On the 30th of January, three pupils who attended a mission-run boarding school for girls, started laughing. What would usually be seen as innocent, became a lot more sincere when the laughter spread to 95 of the school's 159 pupils. Pupils were affected from a few hours to up to 16 days, and the outbreak lasted for around 48 days in total, eventually forcing the school to close.

In the next 18 months, the laughter spread, with villages being affected, 14 schools shutting down, and over 1,000 people catching the 'disease'. The outbreak is thought to have been caused by mass psychogenic illness, potentially triggered by stress and cultural shifts. So really, it was no laughing matter!

# HOW CAN YOU 'BUILD A BRIDGE AND GET OVER IT'?

Well, if you're faced with a problem, the best thing to do is build a bridge. That's what Alexander the Great found to be true, at least! In 332 BC, Alexander orchestrated a siege on Tyre, an island on the Mediterranean with walls up to the sea. These fortifications meant usual methods could not be used, so Alex had to think on his feet.

After blockading and besieging Tyre for seven months, he built a causeway to the island. The causeway was a kilometer-long and two hundred foot wide - and remains there until this day. Once the city was breached, 6,000 fighting men were killed and 2,000 Tyrians were crucified on the beach. So why not give it a try?!

# CAN IT REALLY 'RAIN MEN'?

Well it might have in Kentucky in 1876... during the 'Kentucky meat shower'. For seven minutes, chunks of red meat fell from the sky in a 100-by-50-yard area, near Olympia Springs in Kentucky. There are several different reports of what the meat was, from beef, lamb, horse, and even human...

Though there has been no conclusion on what happened during the meat shower, it's thought it could be from vultures vomiting food in order to make a quick escape. Some people even ate the meat... Vulture vomit, anyone?

# WHERE'S THE CRAZIEST PLACE SOMEONE HAS EVER PEED?

Not many pees will come close to one particular pee taken in 1969. Date ringing a bell? During the Apollo 11 mission to the moon, humanity achieved many firsts: the first men on the moon, and the first proper look at the surface of the moon. A lesser-known first? The first pee taken on the moon - by Buzz Aldrin himself.

Not only did he pee on the moon, but his urine collection device in his suit was broken, so he essentially wet himself. One small step for man, one giant pee for mankind!

# CAN YOU REALLY 'DANCE 'TIL YOU'RE DEAD'?

In Strasbourg, in 1518, the longest-ever impromptu dance party took place. What started with one lady, turned into a whole town affair, with hundreds of people joining in. Bewildered by the dancing chaos, a doctor proclaimed that the irresistible urge to dance was an effect of 'overheated blood' on the brain. The cure? To keep dancing!

Unfortunately, many people kept dancing until they died from exhaustion. It's now thought that the dancing plague may have been caused by a mass psychogenic illness - for which dancing is not a cure, but exhaustion will certainly put and end to.

# DID GENGHIS KAHN HAVE ANY REDEEMING QUALITIES?

Genghis Kahn was the leader of the largest land empire in history, and was responsible for the deaths of as many as 40 million people, reducing the Earth's population by 11% and wiping out entire civilizations. His redeeming property? He was an eco-lover! That's because by killing as many people as the Mongol Empire did, Genghis reduced the carbon in the atmosphere by approximately 700 million tons.

That probably makes him the most effective, and definitely the most murderous, eco-warrior of all time - maybe not a redeeming quality then.

# WHO WOULD WIN A FIGHT BETWEEN ANCIENT EGYPTIANS AND A BUNCH OF CATS?

Ancient Egyptians loved cats and they were all but worshipped due to their close association with the goddess Bastet. They would be mummified and buried with jewelry, whole families would shave their eyebrows to mourn their dead cats, and if someone killed a cat? They'd be killed too.

Unfortunately for the Ancient Egyptians, the Persians caught wind of their devotion, and in the Battle of Pelusium in 525BC the Persian forces not only painted the goddess Bastet on their shields, but also sent cats ahead of them on the frontline. Afraid to injure the kitties, the Egyptian forces retreated, leading to Persian victory and the beginning of Persian rule over Egypt.

# CAN YOU GET REVENGE FROM BEYOND THE GRAVE?

One man certainly achieved just that – Máel Brigte, also known as Máel Bucktoothed because of his protruding teeth. When Sigurd Eysteinsson, a Viking Earl, met Máel on the battlefield, they had agreed to only bring 40 men each. But Sigurd broke the deal and brought 80, killing Máel and all of his men.

Taking Máel's head for himself as a trophy, Sigurd strapped it to his horse. On the ride home, Máel's buckteeth scratched and cut Sigurd's leg; a wound that would eventually become infected and kill Sigurd. It seems it's never too late for revenge!

# WHAT IS THE SH*TTIEST JOB OF ALL TIME?

Henry VIII is best known for his penchant for beheading and divorcing his wives, but did you know he had another strong interest? His bowel movements! So much so, that he had men whose jobs were specifically to monitor his bowel movements, his diet and mealtimes, and help him undress for doing the deed.

The role, known as 'The Groom of the Stool', although seemingly sh*tty, was actually a coveted position as it led to unobstructed access to the King, and often meant they were privy to otherwise unknown secrets. The role continued to exist up until the reign of Edward VII who had it discontinued in 1901.

# HOW CAN YOU GET PEOPLE TO EAT THEIR VEGGIES?

In the 1700s, Antoine-Augustin Parmentier was captured during the Seven Years' War. He was imprisoned in Russia and found himself eating a lot of one certain food: potatoes. But back in his home of France, potatoes were viewed with skepticism: they were only considered food for animals, and were even thought to cause leprosy!

But having experienced the nutritional value of the tuber himself, he came up with a plan to get the food in favor with the French. He planted a field of potatoes and had armed guards stand watch so people thought there was something valuable there. Then, as people do, they started to help themselves!

Thus, the French were tricked into wanting to eat potatoes. Genius!

# HOW FAR COULD YOU FALL WITHOUT A PARACHUTE AND STILL SURVIVE?

The answer might surprise you. With the added help of some pine trees and 18 inches of snow, Flight Sargeant Nicholas Alkemade fell from 18,000 feet in the air, and survived! Even more impressive still was that the only injuries he obtained were a twisted knee and bruising.

He achieved this incredible feat when the Lancaster Bomber he was in was critically damaged by German planes. The pilot of the Alkemade's plane ordered his crew to take their parachutes - but Alkemade's parachute was in flames.

He made the split decision to jump out of the plane anyway, preferring to die on impact with the ground than burn to death. As he fell from 18,000 feet the plane exploded above him, and Alkemade eventually lost consciousness on his descent.

When he awoke, he was relatively unharmed, as his fall had been slowed by flexible branches of pine trees, and 18 inches of fresh snow. Alkemade was rescued by German locals, and after treatment at hospital, he was questioned by the Gestapo who believed him to be a spy - but the discovery of his discarded parachute harness proved his story.

# SHOULD YOU BRING A SWORD TO A GUNFIGHT?

Jack Churchill, also known as 'Mad Jack', became famous for his escapades during World War II. With his motto "Any officer who goes into action without his sword is improperly dressed", Mad Jack was never seen without his sword on the battlefield. He famously kept soldier's spirits high by playing the bagpipes, and there's even footage of him playing it to his unit on a boat after successful raids on Nazi garrisons in Norway.

Awarded the Military Cross for bravery, he also won the Distinguished Service Order (twice) for his command and leadership. So should you bring a sword to a gunfight? Apparently so!

# CAN A PERSON BE A BAD OMEN?

It could definitely be argued that Robert Todd Lincoln, the eldest son of Abraham Lincoln, was a walking bad omen when it came to presidents. That's because he had the unfortunate luck of being present or in the vicinity of not one, not two, but three presidential assassinations.

He was at the White House when his father was assassinated at Ford's Theatre (only a few blocks away). Then, he witnessed the assassination of President James Garfield in 1881, and finally, he was outside of the building in New York when President William McKinley was shot in 1901. After the third incident he seemed to recognize his bad luck and refused a presidential invitation saying, "I'm not going... there is a certain fatality about presidential functions when I am present."

# CAN GREAT PEOPLE BE PETTY?

Well, it turns out that Alexander the Great was also Alexander the Petty! When little Alexander was young he had been scolded by his tutor Leonidas for offering too much frankincense to the gods.

Fast forward to many years later, Alexander had defeated the Persian ruler Darius III and sent 500 talents of frankincense and myrrh (around 17 tons) to Leonidas - apparently with a letter advising him to stop being so stingy in his worship!

# WHAT WOULD HAPPEN IF ALL THE BIRDS DIED?

In 1958, Mao Zedong, the People's Republic of China's founding father, had a bright idea. He decided that his country could do without four key pests: rats, mosquitoes, cockroaches and sparrows. Why sparrows? Well, they ate grain that was meant for people – so he ordered the people to kill them all.

The result of this? A famine that killed up to 45 million people. It turns out that sparrows are a key predator of a more problematic pest: locusts. Without sparrows, the locusts thrived and swarmed the country eating everything in their path - including the grain.

Moral of the story? Don't f*** with nature.

# CAN BEARS JOIN THE ARMY?

During World War II, a Polish Artillery Company adopted an unlikely companion. Whilst in Iran, fighting against Nazi forces, they traded a Swiss Army Knife, canned beef, and chocolate for a Syrian brown bear cub. They named him Wojtek and raised him as one of their own.

Eventually, the outfit were told that they weren't allowed pets in the military, so they formally enlisted Wojtek and gave him the rank of private. Not only acting as a morale booster for the troops, Wojtek also transported artillery shells and ammo crates during the Battle of Monte Cassino in 1944, earning him the rank of corporal.

After the war, Wojtek retired to Edinburgh Zoo, where his former comrades visited him, wrestled with him, and brought him beer!

# WOULD CATS MAKE GOOD SPIES?

In the 1960s, the CIA was desperately looking for new ways to spy on the Soviets. One of the bright ideas they came up with was to enlist the help of one of our four-legged friends: the cat. In an hour-long procedure, a vet implanted a microphone into a cat's ear canal, along with a radio transmitter in the base of its skull. On the first Acoustic Kitty mission, they released the cat to eavesdrop outside the Soviet embassy in Washington D.C.

One story goes that the cat was immediately hit by a taxi and killed, but the 'official' story is that the equipment was removed from the cat as it couldn't be properly trained, and it lived a long and happy life afterwards. Overall, the failed project cost the CIA $20 million - meow!

# WHAT IS MORE UNLIKELY THAN HELL FREEZING OVER?

What about a cavalry unit capturing a fleet of warships? These two military outfits are extremely unlikely to ever meet in battle, but that's what happened when the Dutch fleet was frozen in the Zuiderzee Bay. The cavalry crossed the ice to negotiate with the Dutch fleet, the horses hooves wrapped in fabric to ensure safe passage.

Though previously at war due to the French conquest of the Dutch Republic, the Dutch ships in the harbor had been ordered by their government to stay anchored, and no longer fight the French. After negotiations, it was determined the Dutch fleet would remain at anchor until the political situation was clearer. So, a bunch of horses successfully captured 14 warships!

# CAN A COW BE A BOOTLEGGER?

It's unlikely, but in the Prohibition era, the real bootleggers did their best to make it seem like it!

They did this by wearing shoes with blocks of wood underneath carved to look like cow hooves. This meant that when the police were looking for suspicious activity, instead of seeing human footprints, which might have been a red flag and potentially led them right to the moonshine, they would see cow tracks and think nothing of it!

We can't imagine they used this technique when they were in the city - but it doesn't hurt to try!

# IS MOLASSES BAD FOR YOU?

2.3 million US gallons of it is – as over 170 people found out in Boston, in 1919. A large tank storing molasses burst and rushed through the streets at around 35 mph (56 kph), reaching a peak wave height of 25 feet.

This sticky tsunami killed 21 people and injured 150 others, taking out buildings, tipping over streetcars, and hurling a truck into the harbor.

The cleanup took weeks, with the harbor staying brown until the summer months later. It was also reported that everything in Boston was sticky, and people could still smell molasses on hot days, decades later.

# CAN A PACIFIST JOIN THE ARMY?

Desmond Doss was a Seventh Day Adventist from Virginia, who joined the American Army despite his pacifism. Throughout boot camp, he refused to carry a weapon, and required Saturdays (the Sabbath) to be his day of rest - causing many of his fellow soldiers to bully and threaten him. Despite this, he refused to leave and they were unable to force him.

He made it through boot camp and it was in April 1945 when he proved himself. His battalion had been called to fight near Okinawa, on a island off the coast of Japan. The location was a 400-foot-high cliff, known as Hacksaw Ridge, which the men needed to climb using cargo nets to reach the top, where thousands of Japanese soldiers were waiting in caves and holes.

The campaign was over a month-long, and as a combat medic, Doss treated soldiers on the field, sometimes within meters of the enemy. On one Saturday, Doss joined the rest of the men as he was the only medic available to help, and they were close to taking the ridge.

The battle was extremely bloody, with many Americans being injured or killed. All of the remaining soldiers retreated down the ridge, apart from Doss, who stayed to administer treatment to injured soldiers, then lower them down the cliff. He rescued 75 soldiers that day. He received the Medal of Honor for his efforts.

# HAS ANYONE EVER REALLY 'SAVED THE WORLD'?

It could certainly be argued that two men did during the Cold War. One of them, Stanislav Petrov, prevented nuclear war when he determined an alert from the Soviet nuclear early warning system to be a false alarm.

The system believed 5 intercontinental ballistic missiles were heading toward the Soviet Union, but Petrov decided to not report the alarm to his superiors before he had confirmation, which never came. Due to heightened tensions, if he had raised the alarm, the USSR would likely have launched missiles in retaliation - when the US 'missiles' were actually just a rare alignment of the sunlight on high-altitude clouds.

In Vasily Arkhipov's case, he prevented a Soviet submarine from launching nuclear torpedos at the US Navy, during the Cuban Missile Crisis. American Navy destroyers had located Arkhipov's nuclear-armed submarine near Cuba, and dropped depth charges to force the submarine to come to the surface.

The submarine had received no radio communications for days and did not know if war had broken out. The captain decided it might have, and then wanted to launch a nuclear torpedo. To launch the torpedo, the three officers needed to unanimously agree on the attack. Only Arkhipov remained against the launch, preventing nuclear war. Talk about a close one!

# ARE ZOMBIES REAL?

No, but in 1494 there was the next best thing. During Italy's Renaissance period, sailors returning from the New World brought home a souvenir: syphilis. It spread throughout the French army who then in turn spread the disease through Europe. With no antibiotics, 'the great pox' was able to spread rapidly.

The skin on people's faces would rot away because of the ulcers, with some people's noses rotting away completely, and many people even dying from the disease. So whilst it's not exactly World War Z or The Walking Dead, it probably didn't look too far off!

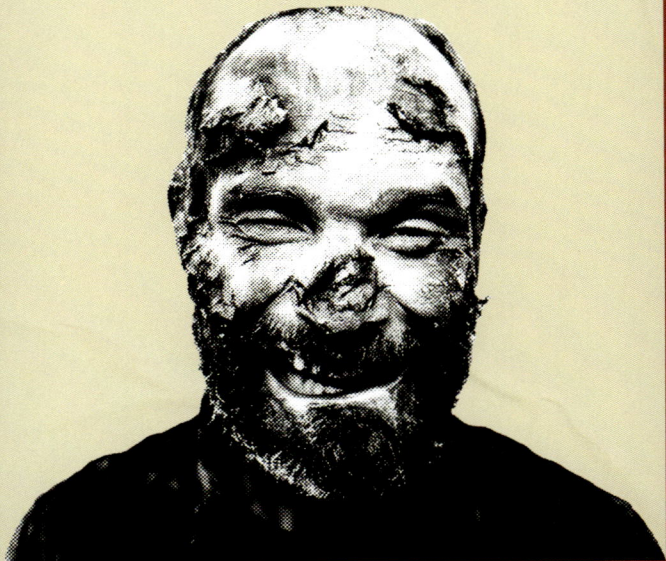

# ARE VAMPIRES REAL?

Again, no, but in Rhode Island in the 1800s they were pretty sure they were. When 'consumption' (what we know as tuberculosis) struck the area, residents thought that surely the victims had been attacked by vampires, since they looked so drained and sunken.

When the members of a family started dying one by one, they assumed that one of the family must be a vampire who was feeding on the others. To confirm their theory, they decided to exhume the bodies. The youngest daughter, Mary, had died later than the others and her body was less decayed, so she was therefore presumed a vampire.

They burned her heart and liver, mixed the ashes with water, then gave this delicious cocktail to someone in the town, to cure them of their disease. Did it work?
No, of course it didn't.

# HOW DO SOLDIERS FIND THE COURAGE TO FIGHT?

Well for soldiers from Nazi Germany in World War Two, the answer was simple: meth! Yes, a pill called Pervitin was the drug of choice for soldiers in the war to help them stay awake through the night, and numb the terror and fear – but it was essentially just methamphetamine.

It wasn't just used on the front lines though - housewives back in Germany used it to finish all their housekeeping and to lose weight! It's no wonder that after the war Germany had a prolific drug problem...

Even Adolf Hitler had his own addiction - to a drug called Eukodal which was a combination of oxycodone and cocaine!

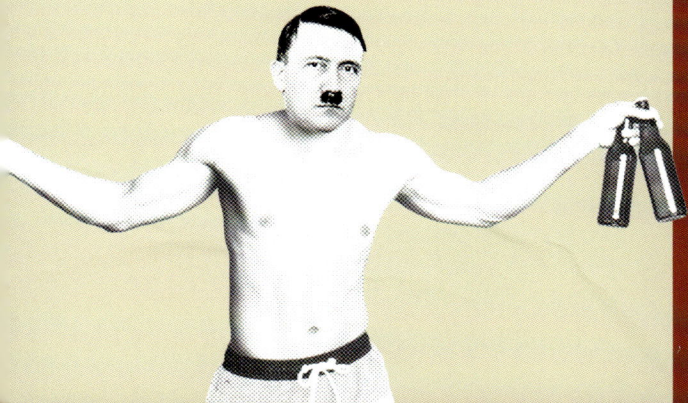

# WHAT COULD 'A LITTLE BIRD' TELL YOU?

Quite a lot, in the case of Commando, the pigeon who served the British Army in World War Two. When radio communications were dangerous, pigeons were sent instead with a small canister on their leg which would hold vital information. Oftentimes, these pigeons would meet miserable ends: either shot out of the sky, set upon by German falconers, killed by bad weather, or wild birds of prey. This meant that less than 1 in 8 pigeon missions were successful.

Commando was clearly made of something different, though, as he successfully carried out over 90 missions for the Brits, including several transmitting crucial intelligence from within occupied France. This information was able to inform the Allied forces of the locations of German soldiers, industrial sites, and injured British troops. For his efforts, Commando was awarded the PDSA Dickin Medal - the animal equivalent to the Victoria Cross.

# ARE DOGS ACTUALLY THAT LOYAL?

We've all heard the comparison 'as loyal as a dog' and the phrase 'man's best friend' but is it true? It definitely was for one dog named Hachikō. Born in 1923, Hachikō was an Akita owned by Hidesaburō Ueno, a university professor in Japan. Every day, when Ueno returned from work, Hachikō would meet him at the train station. That was until one day, when Ueno didn't return as he suffered a cerebral hemorrhage whilst giving a lecture and died. But that day, the same as always, Hachikō waited for him to get off the train. That day, and every day for the next 10 years.

After articles were published about Hachikō, he became famous and people would bring him treats as he loyally waited. Hachikō died at the age of 11 from terminal cancer, and not once during those 11 years did his loyalty falter. His ashes are buried next to his owners, so they may rest together, and statues around Japan commemorate him and his unwavering loyalty.

# WHAT COULD HAPPEN IF YOU'RE MISDIAGNOSED?

Albert Stevens was a house painter who checked into the University of California Hospital in San Francisco with a gastric ulcer. Unfortunately for Stevens, his ulcer was misdiagnosed as terminal stomach cancer, and he was volunteered for human experiments involving radiation, completely unbeknownst to himself. He was injected with a mixture of plutonium isotopes and had tests conducted on his tissue, urine, and stool samples throughout the rest of his life - something he was told was because of his remarkable 'recovery' from his stomach cancer surgery.

Yearly he received over 60 times the allowed whole-body dose permitted to radiation workers in the USA. Stevens never knew that he was the subject of human testing, or even that he never had cancer in the first place (which was discovered during his surgery), and died of heart disease 20 years later. He is now remembered as the most radioactive human ever.

# CAN YOU LAUGH IN THE FACE OF DEATH?

Saint Lawrence was a deacon who helped the poor and needy under Pope Sixtus II. When Sixtus was condemned to death, he told Lawrence to not worry, as Lawrence would follow him in three days. Overjoyed, Lawrence gave all his money away to the poor people of the city.

The Prefect condemned Lawrence to a slow and cruel death: he was tied on top of an iron grill over a fire, slowly roasting him to death. But Lawrence couldn't feel the flames as he was apparently filled with the love of God – he even joked "I'm well done on this side. Turn me over!" From there, St Lawrence became the patron saint of cooks, poor people and comedians, to name a few!

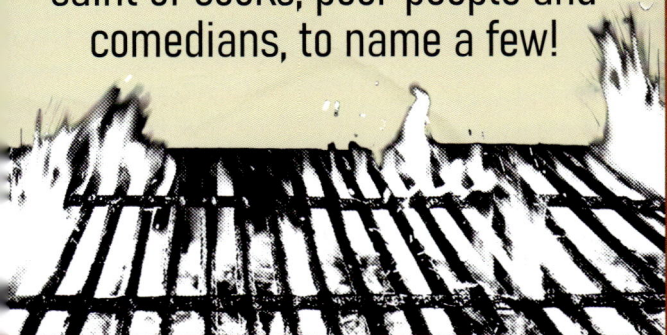

# IS REVENGE REALLY A DISH BEST SERVED COLD?

Not in the case of Olga of Kyiv. When the Drevlian tribe stopped paying tribute to Prince Igor, Olga's husband, he traveled to see why. There they tortured him horrifically, apparently ripping his body in half. As the now regent of Kievan Rus, Olga vowed revenge against the Drevlians.

Prince Mal of the Drevlians proposed to Olga, wanting to gain control of Kievan Rus territory through the marriage. He sent twenty dignitaries to her, hoping they would convince her of the marriage. Instead she had her soldiers dig a ditch, which they threw the dignitaries in, then burying them alive.

But she didn't stop there, before Mal heard of the news, Olga traveled to the Drevlian capital, and hosted a funeral banquet for her husband, inviting Drevlian soldiers to show good faith. Once drunk, over 5,000 Drevlian men were slaughtered by Olga's soldiers. Despite pleas to return to Kyiv, Olga laid siege to the capital for over a year.

Eventually, Olga offered them peace, for a tribute of three pigeons and sparrows from each house. Once received, she had her soldiers tie a piece of sulfur to each bird with cloth, then released them back to their homes. When the birds landed on the houses, they were set alight, burning all of the houses to the ground. So for Olga, it seems revenge was a dish best served hot.

# WHY WOULD YOU 'SHOW SOMEONE WHAT YOU'RE MADE OF'?

In Abraham Lincoln's case, it saved a man's life! When Abraham Lincoln wrote a letter to a newspaper under a fake name, slandering his political opponent, it did not go down well. When the opponent, James Shields, found out the true identity of his naysayer, he wrote a letter in return, demanding an apology or there would be "consequences" - which back then, could only mean a duel! After several more angry letters were sent between them, a duel was organized.

As the one being challenged, Lincoln was able to set the rules: the duel was to be fought with swords. When they were getting ready for the duel, Lincoln swung the sword over his head and chopped off a high tree branch. This was enough proof of Lincoln's strength for Shields and he immediately called for a truce. So show them what you're made of – you might avoid a fight to the death!

# WHO WOULD WIN A FIGHT BETWEEN AN OSTRICH AND A GRIZZLY BEAR?

We don't even need a historical reference to answer this one, it's quite obvious the bear will take the win... come on...